Copyright © Joy Berry, 2020
Reprinted by permission. Originally Published 1987

The statements and opinions expressed in this work are solely those of the author and do not reflect the thoughts or opinions of the publisher.

Every effort has been made to trace the copyright holder(s) and obtain permission to reproduce all elements of this material.

All rights reserved. No part of this book may be reproduced or used in any manner without the prior written permission of the copyright owner, except for the use of brief quotations in a book review. For inquiries or to request permission, contact the publisher at rights@lemurpress.com

ISBN 978-1-63617-032-9

Published by Lemur Press
lemurpress.com

LEMUR PRESS

Mommy and Daddy love me.

But Mommy and Daddy cannot be with me all the time.

Because they do not want to leave me alone, they take me to daycare.

There are special workers at daycare.

They take care of me while Mommy and Daddy are away from me.

At first, I was afraid to go to daycare because Mommy and Daddy would not be there to take care of me.

I learned that the daycare workers could take care of me.

I learned that I could do a lot to take care of myself.

At first, I was afraid to go to daycare because I did not know anyone there.

But soon, I got to know the people at daycare.

Now, they are my friends.

At first, I was afraid to go to the daycare center because I did not know what to do there.

The daycare workers told me everything I needed to know.

Now I know what to do when I am at daycare.

I have fun at daycare. There are many things for me to do there.

When I am hungry, there are good things for me to eat at daycare.

When I am thirsty, there are things for me to drink.

When I am tired, there are places for me to rest at daycare.

Sometimes Mommy and Daddy cannot be with me.

I am glad there is a place where I can go when Mommy and Daddy cannot be with me.

I love daycare!

www.ingramcontent.com/pod-product-compliance
Lightning Source LLC
Chambersburg PA
CBHW081413070526
44583CB00020B/2785

"My goal is to help children of all ages live responsibly, so they can be happy and successful. To accomplish this, I've written books that speak directly to children about things that are happening in their everyday lives. I've tried to make the books entertaining and fun by adding cartoons and humor. As for the age-appropriateness of the books, I've always depended on each parent's judgment and each child's needs, skill level, and interest to determine when a particular book is appropriate for a particular child." —Joy Berry

Joy Berry offers books and media for every age from toddlers to teens, including:

    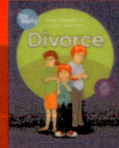 

Teach Me About Ages 1 – 3   **Let's Talk About** Ages 3 – 6   **Help Me Be Good** Ages 4 – 7   **A Fun & Easy Way** Ages 6 – 10   **Good Answers to Tough Questions** Ages 6 – 12   **Winning Skills** Ages 11 and up

Copyright © Joy Berry, 2020
Reprinted by permission based on 2020 Published Edition

All rights reserved. No part of this book may be reproduced or used in any manner without the prior written permission of the copyright owner, except for the use of brief quotations in a book review. For inquiries or to request permission, contact the publisher at rights@lemurpress.com

Cover Design & Art Direction: John Bellaud
Art Production: Geoff Glisson

For more great books and other works by Joy Berry visit **joyberryenterprises.com**

ISBN 978-1-63617-032-9